Edwin Abbott Abbott

Parables for Children

Edwin Abbott Abbott

Parables for Children

ISBN/EAN: 9783337817299

Printed in Europe, USA, Canada, Australia, Japan

Cover: Foto ©Andreas Hilbeck / pixelio.de

More available books at **www.hansebooks.com**

PARABLES

FOR

CHILDREN.

BY

THE REV. E. A. ABBOTT, D.D.

HEAD-MASTER OF THE CITY OF LONDON SCHOOL;
AUTHOR OF "BIBLE LESSONS," "GOOD VOICES," ETC.

WITH ILLUSTRATIONS.

London:

MACMILLAN AND CO.

1873.

LONDON:
R. CLAY, SONS, AND TAYLOR, PRINTERS,
BREAD STREET HILL.

PREFACE.

ANY parents are probably in the habit of reading and explaining some of the simpler parables before allowing their children to read the connected narrative of the Gospels. The titles of some of the following stories, the Bearer of Burdens, the Light of the World, the Broken Branch, the Refiner, will perhaps, in themselves, furnish a sufficient explanation of the Author's purpose, which is, by means of a number of easy stories based on the Metaphors of the New Testament, to prepare young children for the parables or "stories of Jesus," as the best introduction to the detailed history of His Life.

CONTENTS.

viii CONTENTS.

LIST OF ILLUSTRATIONS.

P   B

PARABLES FOR CHILDREN.

 HAVE told you how Jesus lived and died long ago for men, and how He rose from the dead and is now in heaven. Now I wish to tell you of all that He does for you and me every day; how He speaks to us and helps us, and will help us every hour of our lives.

Perhaps you say, "Does He speak to me? And does He help me? How can that be, for I cannot see or hear Him?" My dear child, every good thought you have, and every good deed you do, comes from Jesus, who breathes His goodness into us, and speaks to us continually in our hearts, saying, "Do this; do

B 2

not do that." He speaks to us in many ways. Sometimes, when we read the story of His life, how wise He was, how powerful, how kind, and how infinitely good, we feel that we should like to be good, as He was. Above all, when we think of Him patiently hanging on the cross, dying for each one of us, for you, my dear child, as much as for anyone else, then we feel a desire to be good and kind, as He was. At such times Jesus is speaking to us, and saying, " Come to me, dear child, and let me help you to be like me."

Do not think, then, that Jesus, now that He is in heaven, forgets little children, or cannot speak to them. He is in your heart, always helping you. You see in the picture Jesus suffering for you on the cross; and that picture reminds you how much He did for us eighteen hundred years ago. But you must not think that when He had once done this, eighteen hundred years ago, then He was tired, and wanted to rest from helping us. It is not so. Jesus died, but He lives, and works, and teaches, and helps us as much as ever.

In the Books of the Gospel there are written
many stories that Jesus told His disciples.
He was very fond of speaking about common
things: sometimes about a farmer sowing
seeds; sometimes about a fisherman catching
fish; sometimes about a woman making
bread, or about a number of persons going
out to dine with a friend. Some of these
stories I am going to tell you in easy words.

But do not think that Jesus told these
stories once to other people that lived long
ago, and now tells them no more to you.
Whenever you see these common things about
which Jesus spoke once, He speaks to you
still, repeating the old stories, and He also
tells you new stories. Year by year, as men
grow wiser and better, and as we find out
more and more of God's goodness and power
and wisdom, Jesus speaks to us, telling new
stories about God and heaven.

I wish you always to think of Jesus as a
friend speaking to you every day. We do
not like to draw a picture of Jesus in heaven,
because we do not quite know how He would

appear; so we draw pictures of Him as He died many hundred years ago on the cross. There is no harm in this: it does us good to see the picture of Jesus on the cross. But sometimes, through often looking at this picture, while we think how He died for us long ago, we do not think enough how He lives for us and helps us now. So, whenever you see the picture of our Saviour on the cross, which is at the beginning of this chapter, remember to say to yourself, " He is not dead, but alive: He is speaking to me at this moment, and trying to make me love Him."

PARABLES.

HEN Jesus our Saviour began to teach men about God, there were many things in His teaching that men could not understand. He spoke to men about God, about His goodness and truth, and about the spirits of men; how God wishes all men

to be made like Himself. But men did not understand.

Why could they not understand Jesus? Partly, I think, because they would not think about what Jesus told them : but partly also because they could not see with their eyes the things of which Jesus used to speak. No man has seen God at any time, nor can any man ever see God's truth or goodness ; nor can we even see our own souls or spirits. So, when Jesus spoke about these things, men listened, but they did not think, or understand, for they did not know God in their hearts, and with their eyes they could not know Him.

When Jesus perceived this, He began to teach people in a different way. He noticed that people understood Him when He spoke about things that we see : such as bread for instance, and wine, corn, and the sun, and flowers; and He began to tell people stories about these common things, in order that, if they would think a little, these common things might guide them up to the knowledge of greater things.

I will explain what I mean. Suppose you and your father were walking in the middle of a park, and you asked your father what was the shape of the park. He could not shew it to you, for the park wall would be so far off, that, if you saw one part of it, you could not see the whole; and perhaps, from the place where you were, you could not see any of it. But your father might take his stick and draw on the gravel walk a line running round in the same way in which the park wall runs round; and, from seeing that small figure, you would be able to understand pretty well the shape or figure of the park.

Now, in the same way, God's truth and goodness and love are infinite; they surround us on every side: but they stretch out so far away that we cannot understand them. So, just as your father might draw the shape of the large park in a small figure on the gravel walk, in the same way Jesus shewed men small shapes and figures that would help them to understand the great goodness of God.

For instance, we cannot understand God's great love for us; but Jesus said to us, "You all know how a father loves his children; well, in the same way God loves you, and you may say to Him, 'Our Father.'" Again, God sends His truth into our souls. We cannot see that truth with our eyes, but Jesus points to the sun, or even to a common candle, and says : "As that candle gives light to your eyes, and prevents you from losing your way, so God's truth gives light to your souls, and prevents you from going wrong; and so, God's truth is the light of the world." Again, God sends strength and health to our souls. We cannot see or taste what He gives us to make our souls strong and healthy; but Jesus says to us, "Just as bread and other food gives strength and health to your bodies, so the knowledge of God gives strength and health to your souls." You cannot quite understand this; but you will understand a little of it now, and, as you grow older, you will understand more.

Here is one more of the "small figures"

by which Jesus explained the great shapes
of the things in heaven, and this, I think,
you can quite understand. God scatters His
truths into our hearts. How He scatters it
we do not know, and what it does in our
hearts we do not know. But Jesus points to
a farmer or gardener sowing seeds, and He
says to us, " As a gardener sows seed in his
garden, so God sows truth in your hearts; and
as the seed grows up into a flower, so truth
sown in the heart grows up into actions."

And thus, you see, the parents that live
with us every day, the bread that we taste at
every meal, and even such common things as
garden seeds, are so many "small figures;"
and, just as the "small figure" in the gravel
walk helped the child to understand the shape
of the park wall, so these "small figures"
help us to understand the vast circle of God's
dealings with us.

But nothing on earth can teach us all about
God's goodness : and this I shall shew you in
my next story.

THE SHADOW ON THE WALL.

 LITTLE boy was lying ill in bed at school. He had been ill for a long time; so ill, that he did not know what he said or did. Now, after many days of illness, he opened his eyes and began to think. At first he did not know where he was, and he began to think he was at his old home in India, where he was born, and where his parents were living, far away from him. But as he lay on one side, he saw some of the furniture which reminded him that he was not in his old home, but at school in England. Then he began to think of his home and of his parents, and how much he should like to see them.

While he was thinking in this way, he heard the sound of some one coming very quietly into the room behind him, and he saw a shadow on the wall. He tried to turn round to see who it was, but he found he could not move : he was so weak with his long illness. He felt so weak and dull and quiet, that he did not want even to speak or ask who was there. So he lay quite still, with his eyes wide open, and began to watch the shadow.

He could see the shadow of the face and of two hands moving as though they were at work ; and he also saw the shadows of two knitting-needles, and heard a sound like knitting. So he knew it must be the shadow of a girl or a woman.

Then he looked at the face, and tried to fancy from the shadow what the real face would be like. Every now and then the hand stopped working, and the face looked up and kept quite still as if it were listening. At such times he could see the side of the face, the nose and chin, and forehead, very clearly on the wall : but of course he could not see the eyes or lips, or the expression of the features, and he said, " The face seems rather hard ; I do not think I shall like her. I wish I could have my mother to take care of me instead of a servant."

All of a sudden he remembered that, some time before he fell ill, a letter had come saying that his mother was coming to see him; and now he began to wonder when his mother would come, and how his mother would look. People had told him that his mother would find him changed, because he was only six years old when she last saw him, and now he was ten. So he thought, " If he was changed, would his mother be changed also? Once she was kind and gentle, and tender, and kindness seemed to look out of her eyes. Would she look cold and hard now, like that shadow?"

And now, while thinking of his mother, he remembered that, only the day before he fell ill, he had been expecting his mother to come to the school, and it flashed across him that perhaps she had come, and perhaps she was now in the room, and it was her shadow that he saw. In a moment his eyes filled with tears, and he began to sob with sorrow, and cried out, " If my mother is like the shadow, she will not love me as she loved me once."

The next moment his mother had come round to the other side of the bed, and put her arms round him and kissed him, looking as bright and beautiful and as kind as ever. She did not say a word to him, nor did he to her, for they were too glad to speak; but always after this, as long as he lived, the little boy remembered that though the shadow shews us something, it does not shew us everything.

A good man or woman is a shadow of the infinitely good God. But, just as a shadow has not the look of life that belongs to men and women, and does not tell us everything about them, so even the best man or woman cannot tell us how good and kind God is. Sometimes, when we see that good men are not quite good, we think that God is not quite good, and does not love us. This is a mistake. When we go to heaven we shall no longer see shadows, but the real Father, and we shall be sure that He loves us.

THE SEED.

NCE upon a time a gardener went out into his garden to sow seed. Some of the seed dropped by accident on the hard gravel walks, where it could not sink into the earth : so the sparrows hopped down and pecked it up.

Some of the seed fell near the gravel walk, where there was a little mould, but not much ; and it sprang up in a single night. But it had not earth enough to take root in : so it was soon scorched up by the sun.

Some fell among weeds, and when the weeds and seeds grew up together, the seeds were covered up by the weeds and became weak and thin, so that they never flowered.

Some fell on the garden mould where there were no weeds : and these seeds sprang up, and each seed grew up to be a plant by itself, strong and tall, and put forth first leaves, then flowers, and then pods full of seeds.

When the seeds were gathered in the autumn, there were many more than had been sown in the spring. One plant had as many as ten pods, each with ten seeds in it; so, you see, that seed gave the gardener a hundred seeds. Another had six pods, with sixty seeds, and another gave fifty seeds : and every seed that had fallen on the mould where there were no weeds, gave the gardener more than one seed back again.

Jesus sows His seed every day in our hearts. He speaks to us by our parents, by our books, and in other ways. He says to us quietly in our hearts : " Be kind to your brothers and sisters," " Obey your father and mother," " Do your lessons well," " Do not be greedy," " Never tell a lie."

These little messages are His seeds that He sows in our hearts. But some children will not listen to Him; they make their hearts hard like pavement or like a hard road, so

that the seed cannot sink in. So there lies
the message idle, till some game or some work
drives it out of their minds, and so the message is gone before they have thought about
it. These children are like the gravel walk.

Some children think a little, but not enough.
They hear Jesus saying, " Do not be selfish, do
not be ill-tempered," and they say at once, " I
will do as Jesus tells me." But then presently
they find it very hard to give up their toys and
pleasures for others, and sometimes they are
laughed at by their schoolfellows for not doing
like the rest. Then, just as the sun scorches
up the seeds, in the same way the laughter
makes all their good resolutions wither. These
children are like the earth where there was not
much mould.

Other children are not so forgetful. They
remember what Jesus says to them, and think
of it, but they think more of other things.
Their games and pleasures interest them much
more than the messages of Jesus. They hear
a good voice saying, " Obey your father and
mother ;" but they hear a bad voice saying,

P   C

"It is pleasant to do as we like," and the bad voice is louder than the good voice. So by degrees their good thoughts are conquered by their bad thoughts, and become weaker and weaker; and when the time comes that the good thoughts should bring forth the fruit of good deeds, the good thoughts are dead. These children are like the earth filled with seeds.

But some children hear what Jesus says and remember it and think often of it, and try to obey His messages; and they do what is right and good, and Jesus is pleased with them. These children are like the good earth.

I want you to be like these good children. Do not be careless or forgetful when you read the little stories that I am going to tell you, but remember them, and think often of them.

THE GREAT BATTLE.

HERE is a great battle going on every day all round you and in you. You cannot hear it nor see it, any more than you can see the seeds of Jesus flying in the air; but, for all that, the battle is going on.

Look at the picture on the next page. It shows you one of God's good Messengers called Angels, whom He sends to help us when we are in trouble. The good Angel is trampling down a bad Serpent or Dragon. The Dragon is covered with scales as hard as steel, and breathes fiery breath from his mouth, yet he cannot resist the Messenger of God.

Now perhaps you say to yourself, "I never saw the Dragon." That is true; but though you have never seen him, you have felt what mischief he can do to you—not to your body, but to your soul or heart. This Dragon comes to you in different ways: sometimes he is

Ill-temper, sometimes Greediness, sometimes Disobedience, sometimes Falsehood. But, whenever he comes, he is always deceitful and cunning, and that is why the picture makes him a Dragon or Serpent. He cannot easily be conquered or killed ; and that is why the picture gives him those scales as hard as steel.

Well, then, remember that whenever you are tempted to be unkind to your brothers and sisters, or disobedient to your parents, or greedy, or untruthful, or dishonest, there is the bad Serpent close to you, trying to do you a mischief. If you do as the Serpent wishes, if you are unkind or disobedient, or the like, then you give yourself up to that ugly cruel Serpent. I am sure you do not want to do that. Then what must you do ? I will tell you.

Do you think you can conquer that scaly Serpent by yourself ? You cannot. So you must ask Jesus to help you, and to send one of His golden-winged Angels from heaven to trample down the Dragon. You cannot see the Angels any more than you can see the

Dragon, but, though you cannot see them, they can help you. There are different Angels— Truth, for instance, and Love ; and one of the best of them is Faith or Trust, who helps us to trust in Jesus, and to be quite sure that Jesus is good and strong, and that He will always hear us and help us.

Think often of this. We are all fighting for Jesus against the Serpent. When a little boy tells a lie, he is like a deserter ; he goes over to the side of the Serpent, and fights against his own General. Whenever we are kind and truthful and industrious, we are fighting for Jesus.

This Serpent is called the Slanderer or Devil, because, owing to the Slanderer, men think ill of God, and are afraid of Him instead of loving Him. The Devil tries to make us believe that God is not good, not even so good as a good man. But God is determined that we shall love him. The battle against the Devil has gone on and perhaps will go on for thousands of years ; but in the end the power of the Devil will be quite destroyed.

THE DARK PRISON.

NCE upon a time there was a poor little boy, who had been kept prisoner in a dark room so long that he had become used to the darkness and did not like the light. There was no window in the room; his food was handed up to him through a hole in the floor. The door had been so long closed that brambles and ivy had grown across it.

The poor little prisoner had become so used now to his small dark room that he thought it was as good as a king's palace. The door was not kept locked: but he did not care to open the door and to go out and be free.

At last, while he was asleep one day (for he could not tell the difference between day and night), he awoke and heard a knock at the door. He tried to go to sleep again, but he could not. He tried to keep himself from hearing, by putting his hands to his ears : but the knocking would make itself heard. Then, at last, he felt obliged to get up and go toward the door. As soon as he half opened it, he saw a hand that held a lamp whose light streamed into his dark room. He put his hands to his eyes, and was turning back to his bed in the corner, when he caught sight of the face of the person holding the lamp. The face seemed to say, "Please come out; I have been waiting for you a very, very long time." So he stepped out.

At first the sunlight seemed too bright, and the fresh air too chill, and the songs of the birds too loud. He looked back into his room, half wishing to return. But when he saw his prison by the light of day, it seemed so small and dismal and dirty that he felt ashamed that he had ever liked it ; and after breathing the fresh air he found the air of his old room so foul that he could not bear it, and he wondered how he could have been content to live there so long. So he bade good-bye to the prison, and never came back there again.

Perhaps you say to yourself, " What has this to do with me ? I am not in the dark : I am not a prisoner."

It is true your body is not in prison, but what if your soul is ? What if you are greedy and unkind and untruthful ? If you are, you are in prison ; for you are shut in with unkindness and greediness and untruthfulness. They are like walls, and you cannot get out of them, and you are so accustomed to them that you are contented with your horrible prison.

Then Jesus comes to our heart. " Think of me," He says to us. Sometimes we do not like to listen to Him, or to think of Him. But Jesus is patient ; so He keeps on saying to us, " Listen to me ; think of me." Then when we think of Him, how good He is, how kind and gentle, how truthful and honest, we are ashamed and sorry and disturbed, because we are so unlike Him. We did not know how bad we were till we thought of Jesus. Sometimes we feel as though we should like to run back again away from Him, and be let alone in our badness. But Jesus will lead us onward out of all our faults into goodness and truth. Then when we are free, we shall look back and wonder how we could be content so long to keep away from Jesus in the prison of our faults.

THE SUN'S WARNING.

HERE was once a man that led a very unhealthy life. He would scarcely ever walk out or ride in the open air to see the fields and flowers, but stopped indoors, poring all day, and a great part of the night, over books and papers, so that at last his doctor said to him, " If you go on like this, your eyesight will soon fail." But the man, instead of believing him, went on just as before.

In time he found he could not read his books so easily as before. But instead of blaming himself, he blamed the books, and said, " I don't think people print so clearly as they used to print when I was a boy, and the printing

of my old books seems to fade somehow."
Presently he found that pictures seemed less
distinct than before, almost as though they
were all of one colour. But, instead of blaming
himself, he blamed the pictures, and said,
" People do not paint pictures as they used to ;
and the old pictures fade and change colour
so that one would hardly know them again."
Then, when his friends called to see him, he
used to say to them, " How is it that you look
so changed? You are not so fresh and bright-
looking as you used to be, but dull and grey."
Sometimes his friends answered, " It is not
we that are changed, it is your eyesight that
is growing weak." But he only laughed at
them.

At last, one bright spring afternoon, he went
out into the fields, which were all gay with
cowslips and blue hyacinths and all the flowers
of June. He looked at them and picked a few,
and said to himself, " It is very strange : somehow the flowers do not seem so bright and
clear as they seemed once. They smell as
sweet as ever, but their colour seems faded."

While he said this he happened to glance up
at the sun, and the thought suddenly came
into his mind, " Why, even the glorious sun
seems dull to me; but the sun cannot have
changed, so it must be my eyes that are in
fault, and I fear I am growing blind."

Poor man! How sadly he went home! But
his sadness was good for him in the end, for
he went at once to the doctor, and whatever
the doctor told him to do, that he did; and
fortunately it was not too late, and his eyesight, instead of becoming worse, became much
better. But if the sun had not told the poor
man that he was growing blind, he might have
gone on in his bad habits till it was too late,
and then perhaps he would have been blind
for ever.

As we see the sun with our eyes, so we can
see goodness with our soul or spirit. But as
we destroy our eyesight by bad habits, so by
unkindness, falsehood, and dishonesty our souls
are darkened and cannot see goodness so

clearly. Then sometimes we find fault, not with ourselves, but with other people and things around us, just as the man in the story found fault with the books and pictures. In the same way, we say, " Our friends are unkind and selfish," when, all the while, it is often we that are unkind and selfish.

Then, just as the sun warned the foolish man, so God warns us. God shews us His goodness, and makes us feel how blind and bad we are. This pains us ; but it is good for us, and God pains us to make us better.

Remember that you cannot see goodness in others unless you are good yourself. Jesus said, " Blessed are the pure in heart, for they shall see God," and it is also true to say, " Blessed are the pure in heart, for they shall see God's goodness in all men and women, who are made in the image of God."

THE GOOD SHEPHERD.

NCE there was a flock of sheep in a little green field shut in by a hedge. There was plenty of good grass in the field, and a pond of clear water to drink, and the good shepherd had taken pains to stop all the large gaps in the hedge, that the sheep might not easily get out.

But one day a foolish little lamb said to itself, "Why should we not go outside where the grass is better? I will try to get out." So he managed to squeeze his way through a very small hole in the hedge. When he came to eat the grass outside, he found it was not so good as he expected; so he said, "I will go a little further; I know the way back, and can go home whenever I like." So on he went, further and further, and at last he strayed into a dark wood.

Here he quite lost his way, and, while he was trying to find it, the night came on. Now he began to wish himself safe back in his little field, and he could not help giving a little bleat for sorrow. Immediately he heard a wolf howl close to him, and in another minute the savage beast was upon him. Now indeed he bleated in good earnest; but he would have been torn to pieces if the good shepherd had not been passing by. The shepherd had heard him bleat the first time, and had run up to help him. So he attacked the wolf, and, though the wolf bit him, he drove the wolf away, and took up the little lamb in his arms and carried him tenderly back to the little field, telling him not to stray any more.

Jesus is the Good Shepherd ; the wolf is the Evil One; we are the sheep, and our little field is our duty. When we stray from our duty and do what we ought not to do, we put ourselves in the way of the Evil One.

But if we pray to Jesus, He will help us and

bring us back safe. We ought not to be discouraged if sometimes we stray from our duty. We must try to do better next time, and we must ask Jesus to guide us; but we must not be discouraged, for Jesus himself said, "I have come to save those that are lost."

THE BEARER OF BURDENS.

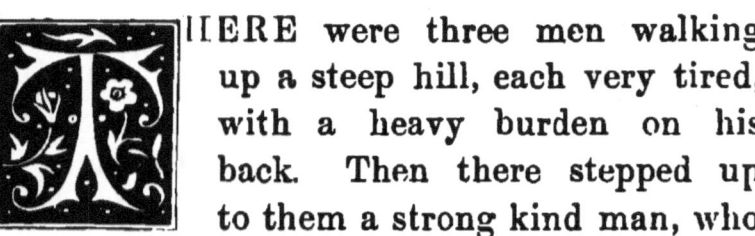HERE were three men walking up a steep hill, each very tired, with a heavy burden on his back. Then there stepped up to them a strong kind man, who said to them, "Let me take your burdens; I will carry them for you." But the first man said, "I have no burden," for he had carried his burden so long that it seemed like his clothes, or like part of his body, so that he did not feel it, and did not know how much better he could walk without it. So the first man would not have his burden touched.

The second man was very selfish and unkind

himself, and he thought all other people must
be selfish and unkind, so he said, "You want
to play me some trick; I do not believe you
want to carry my burden; I will not let you
touch it."

The third man was very tired indeed, and
was saying to himself, "Oh, who can help me ?
for I feel that I cannot carry this terrible
weight any further;" and when he felt the
stranger touch him on the shoulder, and offer
to take his burden, he said at once, "It is very
kind of you; I am very thankful; please take
it, for I see you can bear it and I cannot."

The strong man is Jesus. The burden is
Sin.

If we do not feel our sin, Jesus cannot bear
it for us.

If we do not trust in Him, He cannot
bear it.

But if we are tired of our sins and trust in
Jesus, He will take the terrible weight of our
sins away.

P   D

JESUS THE GUIDE.

N army was once marching to attack a castle, when night came on. It became so dark that a man could scarcely see a yard from his face. So the men stumbled up against one another and fell, and others trampled on those that had fallen. Then many began to quarrel amongst themselves and flung themselves down on the ground in despair, and others wandered off from the rest and tried to find the way for themselves.

But the enemy had dug pitfalls here and there, and had set traps and laid mines, and many of the wandering soldiers fell into the traps and pitfalls. Then they were in great terror : first one said, " I know the way ; follow me ;" then another said, " No, but follow me ; I know it better;" but none of the men really knew the right way, and they only led those that followed them into worse mischief.

At last came up the real guide, with a lantern in his hand, and he said, " Be still, all of you : I will go on before, with my lantern; you must keep your eyes fixed on it, and follow it, and it will lead you rightly."

Then he went on before them, and, though the lantern was but a small one, it shone out so brightly that it lit up all the country round : and the soldiers could now see all the traps and pitfalls, and, besides, they could see each other distinctly and knew what their neighbours were doing, just as though it had been daylight; and they no longer stumbled up against each other, but all marched on in order, keeping step as they went. Then they very soon came to the enemy's castle.

The siege lasted a long time, but in the end the castle was taken and utterly destroyed.

The castle is Sin. All Christians make war against sin. Some children may think that

D 2

they can guide themselves and others in the right way without Jesus : but they cannot. Jesus is the real guide, and the lantern is Christian love. One of the best friends of Jesus wrote in a book that "if we love one another, we walk in the light, and there is no occasion for stumbling." If we do not love one another, then we shall be perpetually offending and stumbling against our neighbours.

THE BREAKER OF CHAINS.

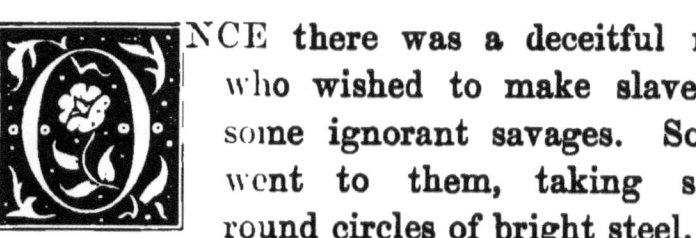NCE there was a deceitful man who wished to make slaves of some ignorant savages. So he went to them, taking some round circles of bright steel, and he said to them, "Put these bracelets on your arms." The poor creatures thought they were pretty ornaments, and they gladly put them on. Now, these bracelets were not really bracelets, but handcuffs made to fasten prisoners with. So, when the Deceiver had once

got the men in his power, he said, "Now put on these pretty chains on your ankles, and these on your legs, and this big chain round your neck."

Then most of the ignorant men obeyed him gladly, and went on putting on the chains : but some said, "No, we have had enough ; these chains on our wrists cramp us : take them off again." But he laughed at them, and answered, "You should have thought of that before ; now you are in my power and *must* do as I bid : put on these other chains, or I will make you." So all the wretched slaves (for they were slaves now) did as they were bid, and made themselves more and more completely slaves. And the worst of it all was, that when the Deceiver had them completely in his power, he set them to work at making more chains for other people.

Many and many a time the poor men struggled to get free, but all in vain ; and many a time people came with large hammers and huge stones and tried to break the chains : but it was all to no purpose. The hammers and stones made a great noise, but they broke nothing; and the Deceiver only laughed at them.

At last there came One bringing a bag full of files, and he offered one to each prisoner. Some of the prisoners were so used to their chains that they liked them, and did not take the files, because they did not want to be free. Another of the prisoners said, "This file is of no use; can this little thing do what the great hammer there could not do? Look at this thick chain round my body; though I worked for a year, I could not break it." So some of them would not take the files; others threw them down after a few moments' trial; others worked patiently away. Those that had only the thin bracelet round their arm soon filed it through (and sometimes the heaviest chain would snap asunder with a touch of the file); others, who had many thick chains, had to work on patiently for years before they were quite free; but, in the end, all that worked gained their freedom.

The Deceiver is Sin, and the chains are Sinful Habits. A bad habit sometimes at first does not seem very wrong. For instance, many a little child will steal a piece of sugar, or tell a falsehood for fun, who would not steal money or tell a serious lie.

When we have once been caught with these little sins, we are loaded with heavier ones. Punishments and warnings do not break us from our sins.

Then Christ comes with the *file*, that is, *love* or *gratitude ;* and if we patiently work away in love for Christ, we shall be freed in time. Sometimes Christ frees us while we are quite little children, sometimes not till we are older; sometimes He frees us suddenly, sometimes not for a long time. The longer we have gone on serving as slaves to Sin, the harder it is to gain our freedom.

THE KING'S SON.

HERE was once a King's son, who heard that the people in one of the King's countries a long way off used to be afraid of the King, and used to say that the King did not care for them. So he thought to himself, "I will go and teach them better." But he said, "If I go with my fine robes and crown, they will say, 'What do you know about a poor man's life? You do not know what it is to be cold and half naked and hungry.' I will put off my royal dress, and I will wear clothes like the poor people, and live and eat as they do."

So he changed his clothes and left his palace, and went to that distant country, and there he lived among the poor, leading a harder life than any of them. And yet, though he was often hungry and cold, and sometimes did not know where to find a night's lodging, he never complained, and never broke the laws.

After he had lived in that country for some time, he went back to the King at home. It happened that soon afterwards the people of the country sent messengers to the King to complain that the laws were too hard. The King's son then said to these messengers, " Believe me the laws are all for the best, and the King loves you as though you were his own children." " Ah," said the messengers, " but you do not understand our way of life, how poor and miserable we are, and how hard it is to live." " You are wrong," said the Prince; " I understand your life quite well, for I lived myself as a poor man among you for a long time. I know you have to suffer a good deal; every one of your troubles is known to me, for I have suffered the same things. Yet still I assure you that the King is very fond of you, and will make you perfectly happy in the end."

Then the people, when they heard that the King's son had lived among them and knew all about their troubles, began to be more hopeful, for they said, "He knows what it is to suffer, and he will surely help us."

The King's son is Jesus, who is the Son of God the Father. Jesus was, as we are, tempted to do wrong. He knew what it was to be poor and hungry and homeless; He felt the bitterness of death. More than this, He knew what it was to be persecuted by enemies, and to be misunderstood and deserted by His dearest friends.

Do not fancy then, when you have your little trials and troubles, that Jesus knows nothing about them and cannot understand them. Jesus was a child, as you are, and He has never forgotten that He was a child. You may tell Him of all your troubles; He will understand and sympathise with them all.

ANGER AND SORROW.

MOTHER was once looking at her children playing together in the garden. Presently one of them came crying indoors. " I know," said the mother, " why you look so angry. Your big cousin took away your hoop, and, when you asked for it, he laughed at you, and, when you tried to take it from him, he struck you in the face, and now he is bowling your hoop and enjoying himself in the garden with the rest, and you have come crying into the house. It is quite right of you to be angry ; but tell me what would you like to have done to your cousin?"

" I should like," said the little boy, " to knock him down and take my hoop away from him." " Very well," said his mother, " I am going out into the garden, and I shall take the hoop away, and I shall punish him also.

But now listen to me a minute. You hope
some day to live with Jesus in heaven : try to
fancy yourself there now. What do you suppose Jesus thinks about your cousin ? You
know Jesus died for all of us, and loves all of
us. He has loved your cousin and taken care
of him ever since he was a baby, just as He
has loved you and taken care of you. Now,
suppose we are close to Jesus, who is sitting
on His golden throne. See, the Angel has
brought that terrible book in which all our
sins are written down, and Jesus sees your
cousin's sin written down there. There are
many other sins written down there, (yours
and mine and other people's,) and this is one
more. But Jesus came to take away all our
sins. What do you think Jesus feels ? I think
He is angry: but is He also glad or sorry ? "
" Very sorry indeed," said the little boy.
" Yes, very sorry ; and if you love Jesus, you
also ought to feel sorry. Now I must go out
and punish your cousin."

" No, mamma," said the little boy; " I
only want him to give me back my hoop, do

not punish him." But his mother kissed him, and answered, " Yes, my dear, I must punish him, not to please you, but to make your cousin know how naughty he has been, and to teach the others not to do as he did. But I am sorry for him, and I shall not punish him more than I can help."

It is right to be angry whenever you see injustice or cruelty, or sin of any kind. For a moment or two, perhaps, you may be so angry that you cannot feel anything but anger. But, remember, you cannot be angry rightly for many moments together with a bad child, unless you feel also sorry for him.

Sorrow is the salt of anger. As salt prevents meat from turning bad, so sorrow prevents anger from becoming a fault.

When you do wrong, how would you like people to be angry with you, and not, at the same time, sorry for you ?

THE QUARRELSOME NEIGHBOURS.

NCE a man built a house in a garden rather near to his neighbour's garden. His neighbour said, "I do not like your house so close to my garden." But the first man said, "I cannot help that; I shall do as I like." Then the neighbour said, "Well, I will make you repent of it; for I will take away your light."

So he set to work and began to build up a tall house quite close to the first house, so as to shut out all the light. Now you must know that the street in which they lived was very narrow indeed, like the streets in old-fashioned cities; so narrow, that you could almost shake hands with the people in the house on the other side of the way. So, you see, hardly any light came to the house from the windows · that looked out into the street in the front, and they wanted all the light they could get from the side. But this quarrelsome man was building up his house so close to his neighbour's house that no light could come from the side.

Every day, while the house was building, the quarrelsome man would come and look at it and say, " Now I shall punish him. Now my enemy will be sorry for having hurt me. How dark and miserable he will be in his new house." Then he would go away rubbing his hands with delight ; and, every week, as the house grew higher and higher, the foolish man exulted more and more and said, " How miserable my neighbour will be ! Who can live without light ? "

Now soon afterwards, just when the house was finished, this quarrelsome man lost almost all his money, and became so poor that he had to leave the fine house in which he was living, and had to come and live in his new house. As soon as the furniture was moved into it, and he had time to look about him, his heart sank within him, when he saw how dark it was, and he said, "I see now I have been very foolish. In taking away my neighbour's light, I have taken away my own, and as long as I live in this house I shall never see the sun."

God's forgiveness is like light to our souls. If we want to take away the light of forgiveness from others, we take it away from ourselves. How is this? I will shew you.

God sees something to love in all men, both in the bad and in the good. If we cannot see something to love in all men, we are not like God. If we go on acting unkindly and unforgivingly, we become more and more unlike God. Then, as we become unlike God, we become afraid of Him and distrustful of Him, and we cannot believe that He loves us and forgives us, and so we cannot be forgiven. Thus, we shut out His forgiveness, as the foolish man shut out the sun-light. Jesus said to us, and still says to us every day, "If you do not forgive one another, your heavenly Father will not forgive you."

THE SHIP WITH TWO PILOTS.

 SHIP'S crew rose in mutiny against the captain soon after they had lost sight of home. Then they said, "Who shall steer us safe to some foreign land?" So they appointed as pilot one of the mutineers, who said he knew the way. But the crew were divided among themselves: some thought the captain knew the way, others believed in the new pilot; at one time the captain's side got the upper hand, and then they used to unbind the captain and set him at the helm: then presently the other side would prevail, and they would push away the captain and put the mutineer in the captain's place. The consequence was, that the vessel used to sail at one time in one way, and at another time in quite the opposite way, so that they made no progress at all.

At last, one evening as the sun was setting,

P   E

one of the oldest and most experienced sailors
said, " Look yonder : there is the Black Rock,
on which hundreds of fine ships have been
wrecked, and we are drifting towards it. Night
is coming on, and the current is taking us fast
to the rock.   This comes of having more than
one pilot."

It is foolish to suppose that we can serve
Jesus at one moment, and Evil the next.
If we do, our life will be a zigzag ; we shall
make no progress, and we may at any moment
run into terrible sin.   Jesus tells us " no man
can serve two masters."

Mind, therefore, you cannot please God on
Sundays and yourselves on week-days.   You
cannot say, " I will do as I am told in school,
but at home I will do as I like ; " or, " I will
try to make my schoolfellows like me, but I
shall not take any trouble about my brothers
and sisters ; " or, " I will never steal money,
but I do not mind taking sugar or biscuits
or a little fruit."   You must try to please
Jesus *always*.

THE TWO ROADS.

HERE is a place where two roads meet. One is broad and smooth, and leads gently down-hill. At first it looks pleasant, and has trees to shade it and flowers in the hedge-rows, but by degrees the trees become fewer, the flowers disappear, the road goes down steeper and steeper, so that you find it harder and harder to turn back; and at last, if you go on, it becomes a straight crumbling cliff, and you find out too late that the road leads nowhere but to destruction, and you slip or fall forward, and are dashed into the sea below.

The other road is so narrow that there is hardly room for two to go together, and it is rough at first and steep up-hill; and for a long way you will find few flowers in it : but if you will only walk on steadily a bit, you

will find it becomes less steep and rough, and
there are flowers in plenty, and at the top of
the hill you will see a beautiful house, with
your father in it, waiting to welcome you.

The broad road is the road of Selfishness;
the narrow road is the road of 'Goodness. At
first it seems easy and pleasant to be selfish,
and hard and painful to be good. But selfishness leads to ruin in the end, while goodness
leads us up to our Father in heaven.

THE ROCK AND THE SAND.

WO men were building their
houses: the first built on a
rock; the second on sand. The
second said to the first, "Why
do you take up so much time in
cutting into hard rock: see how easily I can
drive stakes into this soft sand; my house
will be finished this week, and yours will not
be finished for a month or more."

A month or two afterwards, when the houses were finished, there came a great storm, and the wind blew with all its might, and the rain beat down in torrents, and the stakes were torn up, and the whole house that had been built upon the sand fell down with a crash; but the house on the rock had not a single stake or stone moved, because it was built on the rock.

Jesus is the rock—always the same; and we must trust in Jesus, and obey Jesus, above everything and everybody.

If you trust to anything else above Jesus, you will find that it is mere sand. Everything else will change; but Jesus will never change. Your games and books, that now interest you, will not please you when you are grown up. Your kind friends will grow old and feeble, and will die, and will not be able to help you as they do now. You must always love them and trust them, because, though their faces and bodies may change, they have loved you and always will love you. But remember it was Jesus that gave you these kind friends. So the more you love them, the more you should love Him. Jesus will always be the same, always strong and kind, to the very end of time. If you trust in Jesus, you will do as He bids you. As a house is built on a foundation, so obedience is built on trust.

WATCHING.

 GENERAL, after gaining a great victory, was encamping with his army for the night. He ordered sentinels to be stationed all round the camp as usual. One of the sentinels, as he went to his station, grumbled to himself, and said, "Why could not the General let us have a quiet night's rest for once, after beating the enemy? I'm sure there's nothing to be afraid of."

The man then went to his station, and stood for some time looking about him. It was a bright summer's night, with a harvest moon, but he could see nothing anywhere: so he said, "I am terribly tired. I shall sleep for just five minutes, out of the moonlight, under the shadow of this tree." So he lay down.

Presently he started up, dreaming that some one had pushed a lantern before his eyes, and he found that the moon was shining brightly down on him through a hole in the branches of the tree above him. The next minute an arrow whizzed past his ear, and the whole field before him seemed alive with soldiers in dark-green coats, who sprang up from the ground where they had been silently creeping onward, and rushed towards him.

Fortunately the arrow had missed him; so he shouted aloud to give the alarm, and ran back to some other sentinels. The army was thus saved; and the soldier said, "I shall never forget, as long as I live, that when one is at war one must watch."

Our whole life is a war with Evil. Just after we have conquered it, it sometimes

attacks us when we least expect it. For example, when we have resisted the temptation
to be cross and pettish or disobedient, sometimes when we are thinking "how good we
have been!" comes another sudden temptation, and we are not on our guard, and do not
resist it. Jesus says to us, "Watch and pray,
that ye enter not into temptation."

SAYING AND DOING.

WO brothers used to go to school
together. One evening they
thought they should like to have
a holiday the next day; so they
asked their father to give them
one. He said, "I cannot, because it will put
you back in your studies; so mind you go to
school." One of the brothers said, "Yes, I
will;" but the other said he would not, and
his father was very angry with him.

The next day the one that had said "Yes"
played truant, but the one that had refused

went to school. Then the father said to them in the evening, " Both of you are in the wrong; but you that promised to go and broke your promise are the worse of the two."

Our Father in heaven speaks to us every day, and says, "Do my will;" and whenever we kneel down and say "Thy will be done," we answer God and say " Yes, I will." Now, if we say we will do God's will, and yet do not try to do it, are we not like the boy that first made a promise and then broke it ?

Some people never pray to God at all, and never promise to do His will. Perhaps you are inclined to say, "They are very bad people." But if you promise and do not try to keep your promise, are you not worse than they ?

WAITING AND WORKING.

N army was advancing to fight against the enemy. The enemy was in sight, and the general had begun to draw up his men for the battle. Some he ordered to advance in one direction, others in another; and every one was ready and willing. But turning to one regiment he said, " This regiment must wait here; no man is to stir a step till the order is given."

In a few minutes the battle had begun. Regiment after regiment marched on past the soldiers that were waiting, and very soon all but that one regiment were engaged in the battle. It was hard for the brave men that were waiting, to see their friends march on past them to fight the enemy, and not to be able to march along with them. But at first it was not so very hard; for at first the enemy were beaten back on every side, and shouts of victory came from their friends, and the men in the waiting regiment said, " How lucky they are; they will beat the enemy without us."

But presently all this was changed. Down from the hills behind the enemy, there poured fresh soldiers, who gradually drove back the army step by step. And now the sound of the battle came nearer and nearer, and the men perceived that their friends were being beaten, and it seemed hard indeed to wait. Wounded men were carried past them, whom they knew; and as the enemy pressed nearer still, they could see their friends shot down or run through the body, and that made these brave men almost mad with anger. Presently the shots began to fall among them as they stood close together, and, though the general sent orders to them to lie down, yet some were shot dead without having struck a blow against the enemy. All this was so hard to bear that some of the young soldiers began to murmur, and one of them cried cut,

"Why does he not let us charge? Are we to die lying here like sheep?" But the old soldiers, though they ground their teeth in anger, said, "Be still. We must obey orders. Our general knows what he is about."

The next moment the order came, "Up, and charge." Immediately they leaped up and dashed forward at the enemy. But no more fighting remained to be done, for at the mere sight of these fresh soldiers, the enemy turned and fled, and would not wait till the soldiers could get near them to strike a blow, so the battle was won with hardly any loss.

As they were marching back in triumph, the young soldier that had complained during the battle, said to one of his comrades, "The battle has been won, but we have done nothing to win it; it has been won by our friends, and not by us." But his comrade answered, "You are wrong there; I have fought in a dozen battles before this, and I have never seen anything so hard as this. It is easier to fight than to wait. But after all, whether one fights or waits, it is all one to a good soldier: a soldier's business is to obey orders, and if you obey orders you are doing good service, whether it is your turn to fight or to wait."

Christ our Master has set us all our tasks, and He will come and ask each one of us, some day, "Have you done the task I set you?" If we have done our best at it, He will say, "Come with Me and rest." If we have not done our best at it, He will say, "Depart from Me."

Do not say, "I could do a more difficult work: Jesus has given me nothing to do." Whatever is done for Jesus, though it be only waiting, will please Him. Jesus looks not on the outside, but on the heart. Some children may have done nothing for Jesus, except waiting patiently on a bed of sickness, and bearing pain without complaining. But to all those children Jesus will say, "Come with Me into a place where there is no more pain or sorrow."

Let me end by telling you a short story about *waiting*. One of the greatest poets in the world, named Milton, grew blind as he grew old. His blindness troubled him very much. In his times Englishmen had been fighting against each other, and Milton wished to do what he could to serve God by gaining liberty and peace for England. But he said to himself, "I can do nothing, for God has made me blind;" and he felt inclined to complain against God. Then God said to him, "I do not require work from you that you cannot do. Be patient and wait. If you do that, you will be serving Me. They also serve who only stand and wait."

And while he waited, God taught him wonderful things, which Milton has taught us, and which you must learn when you grow a little older. So it always is. If we are patient and wait for God, God will use us for His glory in the best way.

WILL O' THE WISP.

NCE, when England was not so well cultivated and drained as it now is, travellers by night used sometimes to see, in woods and wet marshy places, a light called Will o' the Wisp. It looked very much like the light of a candle shining from a cottage window.

Once, a poor tired traveller, seeing the Will o' the Wisp, said to himself: "There is the light of a candle yonder; there must be some cottage close by, where I can get a night's lodging." Then he turned out of the right road, and went towards the light; but, when he came close to it, he found himself knee-deep in water, and the light had vanished from its place, and seemed to have moved away. He ran after it, but, the more he ran, he only plunged deeper and deeper into the water, and wandered further and further from the right way.

Now he began to be in great trouble, for he did not know where he was, and he was so tired that he felt as though he could scarcely stir a step further. But he thought of his wife and little children waiting for him at home, and he determined to make one more trial to find his way. He said a short prayer and set out once more. Suddenly another light appeared. He went cautiously up to it. This time, the light did not move. It came from a cottage, where they were very glad to see him, and treated him very kindly, so that early next morning he was able to set out on his journey again, and reached home safely.

———

Jesus is the Light of the World. But He has given some of His light to each of us, just as the sun gives some of his light to the moon. Jesus told us that we are to let our light shine so that other persons may see it. He meant that we are to set others a good example.

If you say your prayers and profess to be a Christian, and yet all the time are unkind and selfish and dishonest, what do you think your little brothers and sisters, who are younger than you, may possibly say? They will say, " Those that love Jesus are no better than others. It is no use to pray to Jesus, for He does not help people. If our brother is selfish, we may be selfish too." Thus you will lead your little brothers and sisters away from Jesus. You will be like the Will o' the Wisp.

How much better to be like the steady light of the cottage candle, that you may lead others right instead of wrong! Here are two lines written by a poet named Shakspeare. Some time or other you will read his books for yourself; but these two lines you can understand and remember now :—

" How far that little candle throws his beams !
So shines a good deed in a naughty world."

THE TRUE WATER.

OME travellers were passing over a dry sandy desert. They were hot and tired, and parched with thirst, and they longed for some water. "See," said the Guide; "look where those three palm-trees rise out of that little patch of grass; there we shall find a little spring oozing out of the ground that will satisfy us all." "That is a mere puddle," said one of the travellers; "it is not enough to satisfy us. Look yonder: there is a vast lake. How odd that we did not notice it before! Let us make haste up to it."

The travellers all turned where he pointed with his finger, and they saw, to their great surprise, a beautiful lake that seemed not far off. They all shouted for joy, and began to run towards it. But the Guide cried, "Stop! I know this country well, and I can tell you that yonder lake is not real water. It is only a pretence, and when you come close to it you will find it will vanish away."

But the travellers said, "Have we not eyes? Can we not see for ourselves? Come, let us leave this lazy Guide, if he will not come with us." So they all ran toward the lake. But when they came close to it, they found it was just as the Guide said. The lake vanished away, and there was nothing but dry sand where they had hoped to find water. Then they were very sorry, and they said, "We ought to have believed the Guide; now we must go back to him."

"Nay," said one of them, "have patience. Look: there is another lake a little further off." They raised their eyes, and, true enough, there lay a beautiful lake that seemed not a mile off. But the wisest of the travellers said, "No, that is perhaps not true water; perhaps it will vanish like the first lake. Let us go back."

So the travellers went back to the spring where they had left the Guide, and when they

came they found the water was enough to
satisfy the thirst of every one of them. But
one foolish man, instead of going back, went
further and further forward, following the
false lake, which kept vanishing whenever he
came near to it. Night came on, and he lay
down all alone, ready to die with thirst. I do
not know what became of him; but I hope
the good Guide found him next day, and
brought him back to the True Water.

Your soul, as well as your body, wants
something to satisfy it. Perhaps you think
you would be satisfied all your life if you had
plenty of toys and pleasant games, or as much
money as you liked; but you would not.
Suppose you had all these things; yet, if all
people disliked you, and you disliked them,
you would not feel satisfied; you would say,
"I do not feel easy; I do not feel at peace."
True peace comes to us when we love all
people like brothers and sisters. Jesus helps
us to love one another, and He alone can give

us true peace. Some people say, "We shall be satisfied and happy if we can get plenty of money, or if we can have houses and gardens and farms, or if we can make people praise us, and say we are clever." But money and houses and praise cannot give us peace. They are like the false lakes. When we get them, we find the peace is not there. It has vanished from its place, and seems to have gone further off. Pray to Jesus and say, "Give us that peace which the world cannot give."

THE STINGING RING.

WO brothers went out to seek their fortunes. When they went to say good-bye to their father, he gave each of them a ring, and said, "Wear this, and whenever you are entering into danger, the ring will sting you: but if you neglect the warning, the sting will grow dull in time and leave off stinging."

The brothers went on their way along the dusty high-road. Presently the elder brother cried, " Look at that beautiful meadow, with long grass and patches of cowslips and wild hyacinths too : we will rest there." They were getting over a stile into the field, when the younger brother said, " Stop, my ring stings me." " So does mine," said the elder brother, " but I must and will have some cowslips."

So on he walked into the middle of the field, picking the flowers as he went, and gathering so large a nosegay that his brother almost wished he had ventured too.

After waiting for two or three minutes, the younger brother said to himself, " There seems to be no danger. I think I will just get over the stile," when, suddenly, in the act of climbing over, he felt his ring sting him sharply again, and, looking round, he saw a long adder winding its way stealthily through the long grass close by him. He drew back, and shouted to his brother, " Here's a snake coming your way." " That cannot be," said the other, still picking the flowers, with his back turned to the snake, "for my ring scarcely stings at all, and I must have a few of these wild hyacinths."

Before he had well uttered these words, the snake had crept up close to him, and it sprang at him and bit him on the leg. Then the poor boy fell to the ground, crying, "Ah! how I wish I had done as the ring told me."

I believe the boy was cured, and did not die of the bite. But he was very ill for a long time, and, as long as he lived, he never afterwards disobeyed the Stinging Ring.

The ring is Conscience, which warns us when we do wrong. Do you know what conscience is? I will tell you.

Whenever we are doing wrong, there is something within us that makes us uneasy, as though we were stung. We cannot hear it with our ears, or see it with our eyes, but we can understand what it means, and we call it *Conscience*.

God has given each one of us a conscience, to warn us against doing wrong. If we neglect its warning, and stray, in spite of it, from the path of duty, the sting of conscience becomes blunted, and we do not feel it; and when Evil comes upon us, we are taken by surprise.

THE BROKEN BRANCH.

 LITTLE branch on an apple-tree was heavy with blossom and young fruit, and seemed as though it would bear a great many apples. It was the most promising branch in all the tree. But one stormy night, being tired of tossing to and fro with the wind, it grew proud and angry, and said, "Why should I hang here among all these barren branches, moving when they move and resting when they rest? They have hardly any fruit themselves, and they hide my fruit. And what do I want with the great useless trunk below that has no fruit upon it?

I should like to come down and grow by myself on the lawn, that all people might see me."

No sooner were these words uttered, than a violent gust of wind whirling through the tree snapped off the discontented branch and dashed it to the ground. A little boy finding it there early next morning, stuck it in the lawn for fun.

"This is capital," thought the branch to itself: "now I shall take root and grow up by myself to be a famous tree." But, alas! when the day grew towards noon, the sun shone with all its heat on the poor branch, and sent a pain right through it from one end to the other, spreading even to every little twig and leaf and blossom.

Now, when it was too late, the poor branch cried out, "Ah! how I wish I had remained on the old trunk. Now I begin to miss the sap and food that the trunk used to send up to me. I am dying with thirst, and all my body is scorching to death."

Just then the master of the garden passed

by, and he said to the gardener, " What a pity that fine branch has fallen—clear it off the lawn at once, and chop it up for firewood."

Every moment in our lives Jesus is helping us to be good. As the trunk gives sap to the branches, so Jesus gives us help to be good. But if we will not trust in Him and pray to Him, but go away from Him and trust in ourselves, we lose the strength that He gives us, and, like the broken branch, we make ourselves fit for nothing but to be destroyed.

Remember that one branch cannot separate itself from the other branches. Your brothers and sisters and friends, and the servants also, are all branches in the tree of Jesus. If you try to separate yourself from them and to think only of pleasing yourself, you are like the foolish broken branch.

THE CHURCH OF UNHEWN STONE.

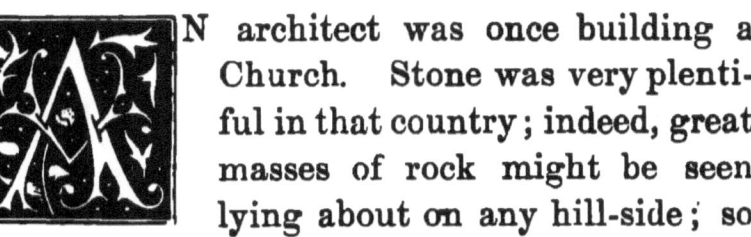N architect was once building a Church. Stone was very plentiful in that country; indeed, great masses of rock might be seen lying about on any hill-side; so there was no need to make brick for the building. So the architect called for his masons and workmen, and said to them, "You will find on those hills close by, a great number of large stones and fragments of rock: use these for the building. Do not cut them equal blocks with flat, square sides, but take them as they are, and make one fit into the other; only you may just trim the stone a little if it is necessary, but you must not cut the stones so as to make them all alike."

Then one of the masons said, "Sir, that will take a long time, and how do we know that all the stones can be made to fit?" But the architect answered: "I do not care how long it takes, and I am quite sure that the stones can all be made to fit, for I have looked at them all myself, and have marked them with chalk: every one of them has its place in the building."

Then another of the masons said, "But if one of these stones is spoiled or slips out of the wall, you will not be able to find one exactly like it, and so it cannot easily be replaced; whereas, if we build with squared stone, we can easily fill up a gap." "True," said the architect, "but you must take care not to spoil one of these stones, and I will take care that none slip out of the wall."

The Church means all faithful Christians, and each stone is a Christian. Jesus changes and shapes us by teaching and by trials, that we may be fit for our several stations; but He does not make us all alike. Hence, no one Christian can fill exactly the same place, or do exactly the same work, as another. There is room for small stones as well as for large, and there is room for rough and jagged stones as well as for smooth square stones in the Church; that is to say, there is room for dull and simple persons as well as for the clever, in the number of faithful Christians: the rich have their places, but the poor have their places also.

You will understand this better when you grow older. Meantime, even though you may be a very little child, you can understand this, that Jesus takes care of all, girls and boys, dull and clever, and gives us all some work to do. Those that are not so clever as others should not be discouraged, but should remember this proverb, " Every stone has its place in the wall."

FIRE.

" W̶HAT a kind friend is fire!" said a little boy, one winter evening. "Fire warms us and makes our rooms look bright and cheerful, and we can take a piece of fire and put it in a lamp, and it gives us light to read, or work, or play."

"Yes," said his father, "and fire helps us in other ways also. Without fire we could not have the poker with which Mamma is stirring the fire, or the steel-pen with which I am writing, or the glass globe of the lamp that gives us light. Fire is a good friend as long as you behave wisely to it; but if you behave unwisely to it, it is not your friend. You must never play with fire, or throw pieces of paper in the fire." "Why not?" said the little boy. "I cannot explain that now," said the father, "for I am very busy; but mind you do as I say, and never play with fire."

That same evening the foolish little boy, when his father and mother were gone out of the room, said, "I should like to have one little game with my friend Mr. Fire, just to know what harm there is in it." So he began to throw pieces of paper into the grate, watching how they caught fire and flew up the chimney. It was great fun for some time; but at last one of the burning pieces of paper out into the room on the carpet. The little boy put his foot on it to stamp it out; but the flame caught his dress, and in a moment he was on fire all over. He shrieked aloud for help, and, fortunately, his father came in just in time to prevent him from being killed. But all his body was scorched, and he was in very great pain, and had to lie in bed for weeks before he could get well.

God gives us many blessings as well as fire: He gives us food, drink, clothes, strength, cleverness. They are His gifts. But if we misuse them, we change God's blessings into curses. If you eat or drink too much, you make yourselves ill; if you are proud of your pretty clothes, you become vain like a peacock; if you think too much of the strength of your body, and of games, you become stupid; if you think too much of your cleverness, you will soon be beaten by other boys that are not so clever as you. Remember that all good things are gifts from God. Then you will be sure to use them rightly. But, if you use them wrongly, they will harm you as the fire harmed the little boy.

Now I am going to say a terrible thing. Even the good Jesus may harm us, if we behave badly to Him. If we read about Him, and will not think about Him, we shall become worse instead of better. If we read about Him, and think about Him, and do not try to imitate Him, we shall become very much worse. If we read how He was kind, and loved us and died for us, and if nevertheless we do not love Him, our hearts will become cruel and hard, harder than they were before we ever heard of Jesus. If we do not like Jesus, we shall be uneasy whenever we think of Him; we shall be afraid of Him, and we shall want Him not to be our friend, but to let us alone.

Jesus will not let us alone. He is a Light, but He is also a Fire. If we behave badly to Him, He will make us uneasy and miserable. He will try to burn out of us all that is bad, that the good may he left. It is good for us to be uneasy and miserable when we are behaving badly. Then perhaps we shall be taught to leave off being bad.

THE REFINER.

HERE was once a little piece of gold lying hid in the earth. It had lain hid so long that it thought it should never be used, and it said to itself, "Why do I lie idle here? Why am I not picked up, that men may see me shine?"

One day a man dug it up and looked at it, and said, "There is some gold in this lump; but I cannot use it as it is; I must take it to the Refiner." When the Refiner got it, he threw it into a melting-pot, and heated his fire to melt the gold. As soon as the little piece of gold felt the heat of the fire, it began to tremble, and cried, "I wish I had lain quiet in the earth." But the fire grew hotter and hotter, till at last the gold melted, and left all the earthy part of the lump by itself.

"Now," said the gold, "my troubles are over: now I shall shine." But its troubles were not over yet. The man took it once more, and began to hammer it into some shape. "Ah!" said the gold, "what a trouble it is to be gold; if I had been dross or common earth, I should not have been put to all this pain." "That is true," replied the man; "if you had been dross, you would not have had all this pain; but then you would not have become what you are now--a beautiful gold ring."

The piece of gold is a little child. The dross or common earth means the child's faults and weaknesses. Jesus is the Refiner: He sends trials and troubles to us to make us good and strong, and to take away our, weaknesses and faults.

Pain is one of a little child's trials. If we bear it patiently, Jesus will make us better by pain. He will make you brave and gentle. Next time when you have to bear pain, say to yourself, " Jesus is taking away my faults: I must be patient."

THE WHEAT AND THE WEEDS.

 FARMER once sowed a field with good wheat. But one night, when everybody was asleep, an envious neighbour came and sowed patches of weeds all over the field. When the wheat grew up, the farmer's servants noticed the weeds growing up

G 2

too, and they came to their master and said,
"Shall we root up the weeds?" But the
master said, "No, for fear you root up the
wheat with the weeds. Wait till the harvest-
time; then the wheat and weeds shall be cut
down together: and the wheat shall be stored
up in the barn, but the weeds shall be burned."

God suffers bad men as well as good men to
live in this world, and to be rich and comfort-
able, and God also suffers good and evil to
remain together in the hearts of men.

But at the last day God will divide the
good from the evil. Then, all that is good
will live for ever, in another world, about the
throne of God; but all that is evil will be
utterly destroyed.

THE WHEAT AND THE CHAFF.

NCE a child that had always lived in a town, went into a barn where some men had been threshing with a flail, and he saw the chaff and wheat lying mixed up together in heaps on the floor. "Look," said the child; "here is a lot of wheat." "No," said the farmer, "it is not all wheat; some of it is not good to eat; it is the mere husk or shell of the wheat, and it is called chaff. Wait a moment till they bring the winnowing machine."

While he was speaking, the men brought the winnowing machine, and set it down at the barn door, and they threw open another barn door opposite to the first, and the wind blew right through the barn, so that there was a great draught from one side of the barn to the other. Then the child saw

how the good heavy wheat remained in the
barn and the light useless chaff was tossed up
into the air and then blown outside the barn,
and he said, "I did not know the difference
between the wheat and the chaff, but the
wind knows better."

Good and bad things and good and bad
men are mixed up together in this world, and
we cannot always tell one from the other : but
God can. Sometimes God winnows and sepa-
rates good men from bad men, even in this
world. I will shew you how.

Once, on board ship, there were two sailors.
One of them was rather quiet, and the other
very noisy and boastful. The second used to
laugh at the first for his quiet ways, and used
to tell long stories about his own bravery and
boldness. So it came to be thought that the
noisy man was very brave, and the quiet man
rather cowardly.

But one night a fire broke out in the ship.
Every one hurried up on to the deck, and the

boats were lowered. There was just room in them for the women and children and a few rowers, but not for all the crew. So the captain said, "Hand on the women and children to the boats." The crew all obeyed. Some of the sailors were ordered to jump into the boats to row. The rest remained in their places. But just as the last boat was nearly filled, and only one woman remained on deck, the noisy sailor rushed before her and tried to leap into the boat. But the quiet sailor, catching the coward by the collar, threw him back upon the deck; then he helped in the poor woman, and bade her good-bye, pushing off the boat from the burning vessel. Thus God winnowed the good from the bad, and the brave from the boastful.

We believe that, in the end of the world, God will winnow all that is bad from all that is good, and will destroy the bad and preserve the good for ever.

THE LETTER.

LITTLE boy, who had always lived at home, was going away for the first time to live at a boarding-school. His father kissed him and said, "Always write me a letter every week, and tell me how you are getting on at school; and if you get into any troubles or difficulties, do not hide them from me, but let me know, and I will write back to you and tell you what you ought to do, and I will let you know all that goes on at home, all about your mother and brothers and sisters, and your little garden, and your rabbits and pigeons."

When the boy found himself at school, at first he felt rather down-hearted, being among strangers and away from his parents, and when he sat down to write his first letter home, he told his father of all his little troubles, and, when he received his father's letter in answer, he was so interested in reading it that he quite forgot he was at school, and he fancied or a moment he was back again at home among his kind friends, and his garden and his rabbits. His father's letter was a great help to him : it told him to be a good scholar in the second place, but a good boy in the first place, and not to mind his schoolfellows' jokes and fun, if they laughed at him for doing right. " If you do what is right," said the letter, "your schoolfellows may laugh at you and tease you at first, and perhaps for a long time, but they will respect you in the end."

But in a week or two he became used to the boys and to his studies, and he liked very well to be at school, and did not so much care to hear from home; and when he sat down to write home, he did not feel that he had much to say; so he began now to write shorter and shorter letters every week, and at last, he forgot to write at all, and when his father's letters came (for his father never forgot to write), he used to pay less and less attention to them, and at last he used to feel annoyed by the good advice in the letter, and he left off reading them at all.

Now, he used not to think much about his father, and he began to fall into idle and bad ways, to cheat in his lessons, and to use bad language. At last he told a lie to his master: and his master punished him, and said to him, " What will your father say when he hears this ? " Then the little boy burst into tears, not because of the punishment, but because he felt he had been very ungrateful and forgetful of his father. That same day he wrote to his father, telling him how sorry he was he had behaved so badly. His father wrote back, forgiving him and saying, " Pray write regularly, for whenever you write you will think of me, and the thought of me may keep you from temptation."

You are that child. Your Father is God in heaven. The letter is Prayer. Pray regularly to God, for God says to you, "Whenever you pray I hear what you say, and I will send you an answer: I shall not answer you aloud, but in your heart."

HOME.

MAN went out to India to live there. He had a very pleasant house, with a large garden, and he and his wife and children lived very happily. At last, as the little children grew up, the heat made them ill, and they became thin and weak, so that one day the doctor said, "If you wish your children to live, you must send them to England."

The poor man could not leave his work in India, so he was obliged to send his wife and children away by themselves, and he was left alone. The day after they had gone away, a friend called upon him and said, "What a pleasant house you have!" "Yes,"

said the poor man, "but it was a home yester-
day; now it is nothing but a house. My home
is where my wife and children are."

Home is not bricks and mortar, nor stone,
but a place where our best friends are.
Heaven is our home, because Jesus, our best
friend, and God our Father, are there.

God wishes all men to think that Heaven is
their home, and so He sends for our parents
and our friends, and takes them away from
our home on earth, that we may be obliged
to look up to heaven and say, "My best
friends are there."

Our best friends are our best treasure, and
Jesus tells us, "Where our treasure is, there
will our heart be also."

NOT SEEING, YET BELIEVING.

NE day a father took his little boy into a large wild-looking garden. There had been no gardener there for a long time, and the weeds had shot up and had choked the flowers and covered over the gravel walks, so that you could scarcely tell the walks from the flower-beds; it was all one mass of weeds. Then the father said, "See, here is a square plot of ground for you ; and take this spade and this rake, this watering-can, and these seeds. Here is some food for you to put in your pocket and to eat when you are hungry. Now set to work, and, after you've weeded the plot, put in the seeds, setting the tall flowers, such as the convolvuluses, behind, and the small low flowers, such as the mignonette, in front. I am going away, and shall leave you here to work all the day through ; but before night comes I shall be

back to see how you have got on. I may be
a little late, but you may be sure I shall come
for you." When he had said this, he went
towards the garden-gate. There was a little
lattice window in the gate looking out into the
road, and this window could be shut by a board,
so that no one could look out. This window
the father shut fast, and then he went out,
locking the gate behind him.

The little fellow set to work with a will,
partly because he loved his father, and partly
because he was fond of work. And for about
an hour the work was very pleasant. He liked
to turn up the big coarse weeds in handfuls,
and to see the mould becoming free from them
and ready for the seeds. But presently he
found the spade was a bit too large for him,
and it shifted about in his hands and blistered
them sadly. He was so vexed that, for a
moment, he could not help saying to himself,
"Why did my father give me this great heavy
spade? It is too big for me." But directly
afterwards he thought, "I can't see why he
did it, but I dare say he did it for the best."

Then, as the day went on, his back began
to ache with so much stooping, and, as the
sun grew higher and hotter, the perspiration
began to stream down his forehead, and he
became thirsty as well as tired, and he said,
"Why did my father give me this plot here
out in the sun, when he might have given
me yonder plot there in the shade of the
trees? I think I will change my plot." But
afterwards he said, "No, I will not change
it. I can't see why he gave me this; but I
dare say he did it for the best."

By this time he had cleared the ground of
the weeds, and had raked it smooth, and was
thinking of putting in the seeds; and now
he said, "Let me see; was I to put in the
tall seeds before and the low seeds behind? or
to put the tall behind and the low before?"
He tried to recollect the exact words of his
father, but they became confused in his mind,
and he could not feel certain what his father
had said. In his trouble he cried out, "How
I wish he had written down what he wanted
me to do! Then I could read the writing and

I should know what to do. Why did not he
write it down?" But then once more he said,
" My father is very wise ; I dare say he did
what is best, though I cannot see it. I will
sit down and try to think which is best, to have
the tall seeds before or behind." So he sat
down and thought a little, and he said, "If
the tall flowers are in front, when they grow
up they will hide the short flowers. That will
never do : so I must put the tall flowers behind
and the short ones in front." Then he took
the major convolvuluses and nasturtiums and
sweet peas, and planted them behind, next to
the wall ; and as for the Virginia stock and
mignonette, he set them in the front.

Now after he had set all his seeds, he took
his watering-can and went to fetch some water
to water the ground. The water came slowly
out of the water-butt, so he was some little
time about it, and, when he came back, he
heard a great fluttering and twittering, and saw
a flock of birds, all busy pecking and scratch-
ing up his neat flower-bed over which he had
taken so much pains ; and one big brown bird,

with spots on his breast—I think it was a thrush—had made a deep hole among the sweet peas, so deep that you could have buried a ball in it. The poor little lad was much vexed at this. "All my work is spoiled," he said, "and what will my father say when he comes back?" and, in his vexation, running to frighten the birds away, he dropped his can and spilt all the water.

Now he was ready to cry, and I think he could have cried, but the brown thrush up in the pear-tree began singing so merrily, that he felt ashamed of crying. But he said to himself, "Why did not my father tell me of these birds? Then I might perhaps have prevented them from coming; or, at least, why did he not shew me how to prevent them from coming? For now I don't know what I shall do. My water is all spilt, and, when I go away to fetch some more, then down will come the brown bird again, and carry away my sweet peas. Yet, after all, my father is wise, and does things for the best. Perhaps I can manage for myself, without waiting till he comes

P   H

to tell me. Let me think. How can I
frighten the birds away?" So, after thinking
a while, he took the pieces of string that had
fastened the seed papers, and tied the seed
papers with their strings to some twigs, and
fixed the twigs in the ground, leaving the
papers all flapping about in the wind. Then
away he went to fetch some more water : and
when he came back, not a bird was to be
seen on the ground, for they were all too
frightened at the papers to come down near
the seeds.

At last, the boy had watered all the seeds,
and put his tools away, and he was ready for
his father to come. But no father came. The
boy had nothing to do now. The sun was just
setting, and it was growing cool and dark, but
still his father did not come. While he was
waiting, it came into his head, "Suppose my
father should have forgotten me, and gone
home without me : and perhaps he may not
remember me till he gets home late at night.
What shall I do here all alone in this cold,
dark place ?" Just at this moment there came

up another boy, who had been working in another part of the garden some way off (for you must know the garden was very large, with lots of shrubs and trees in it, more like a park than a garden), so that our little boy had not seen him. "What!" said the big boy, "are you too waiting here?" "Yes," said the little boy, "I am waiting for my father; he promised me he would come for me." "So he promised me," said the big boy, "but that was early in the morning, and it's getting dark now. I think he must be busy, and won't come now. You had better climb over the wall with me." "That cannot be," said the little boy, "for my father never breaks his promise; he will come, and I must wait." "You stupid fellow," said the other, "perhaps your father has forgotten." "Ah," said the little fellow, "but my father never forgets." "Well," said the other, "if you like being left alone in this dismal place, I don't; so I shall take myself off:" and in another minute he had climbed over the wall and was gone.

H 2

So now the little fellow was quite alone, and very lonely he felt. The birds were all quiet now, and the stars were beginning to peep out, saying that night was coming fast. He went and sat down on the steps that led downwards to the garden gate, to be ready for his father the moment he came in. Then, for the first time, he saw the lattice window in the gate, and said, "That window looks right across the fields along the footpath by which he will come. I will open the lattice, and then I shall be able to see him a long way off, as he comes up." He jumped up, and pushed once and again at the window; but all in vain. The window was fast shut, as fast as the gate itself. "Oh," said the boy, "my father might have left the window open for me; it would have been———" But he had no time to say any more, for the key clicked in the key-hole, and the gate opened, and there was his father; and you may well believe the boy was glad to see him.

"And how has the work got on?" said the father. The boy then led his father to the

plot, and shewed it to him, all clear of weeds,
and raked smooth, and guarded from the birds,
and watered thoroughly. " Well done, my
boy," said the father ; " you shall have this
little plot for yourself, and all the flowers that
come from the seeds you have sown. And how
did you like the work ?" " Very much, father,
at first. But why did you give me such a
large and heavy spade ? Even if I had been
working in the shade, it would have been hard
work : but, as it is, you gave me my plot
right in the hottest part of the garden, and
that made it harder. Look, my hands are
all blistered." " My dear, I knew the spade
would be a little heavy for you at first ; but I
know that in a few days you will find you can
handle this spade easily, and you will be able
to dig better, and your arms will be stronger
than if I had given you a smaller spade. And
if I had given you your plot in the shade, the
work would have been easier, certainly ; but
the flowers would not have grown so well, and
you would not have had so many nosegays as
you will be able to pick from your plot in the

sun. But tell me, did you have any other
troubles; and do you want to ask any more
questions?" "Yes, father. Why did you not
write down how I was to set the seeds? It
took me ten minutes to remember what you
said about putting the tall seeds behind."
"And how did you remember at last?" "I
thought to myself, if the tall flowers are put
in front they will hide the others, so they
must be meant to grow behind, and the short
flowers in front." "My dear boy, that is just
what I wished. You say you *thought:* that's
what I wanted you to do—to think, not to re-
peat what I said, as a parrot repeats things
without understanding them. And I am sure
also you must have *thought,* before you set up
those sticks with the flapping papers to drive
away the birds. I daresay it seemed rather
hard, when you saw the birds pecking at your
seeds; but it has done you good to think for
yourself what is the best thing to do. That
is the way to become a man."

"Well, but one thing more, father. You
must know I was tired of waiting, and, though

I knew you would come because you had promised, yet I felt rather lonely, and I thought I should like to look out of the lattice to see you coming; because the window looks across the fields for half a mile. But, when I tried, I found you had locked the lattice. Then I felt very miserable, and almost ready to cry, and yet all the while you were coming up outside. If I could have seen you, I should not have felt miserable. Would not that have been better?"

"My dear boy, I'm not quite sure that you will understand what I'm going to say; but tell me, did you not believe in me, and feel sure that I would come, although you could not see me coming?" "Yes, I did." "But, if you could have seen me through the lattice, then there would not have been much need for believing?" "No." "Well, then, it is a good thing for children to believe in their parents while they see them; but it is a better thing to believe without seeing. You have done a good day's work. Now we will go home."

The garden is the world; the little plot is our work, which God our Father has given us to do. There are many trials and troubles in this world, of which we do not know the reason; but we trust that our Father sends them for our good, to make us patient, and strong, and wise. Sometimes we are afraid that our Father has forgotten us, and will not take us with Him to our home in heaven. At such times we say, "How much better it would be if we could see Him, and knew that He was taking care of us. Then we should always believe in Him." But God says, "I do not want you to see Me with your eyes. I want you to trust in Me without seeing." And Jesus said to us, and says to us every day, "Blessed are they that have not seen, and yet have believed."

THE BOY THAT HELPED THE KING.

HERE was a little shepherd-boy that kept his sheep down in a lonely valley. War was raging in the land, and the boy would have liked to go out and fight against the enemy; but he was too young. He was a good boy; careful of his sheep and kind to his dog, and active and industrious at his work; and at home he was obedient and gentle, and always ready to do a good turn for anyone. But though he liked his work, he would have liked better to fight, and he was very sorry that he could not be a soldier.

One day a long column of horse soldiers, with bright red coats and flashing helmets, and trumpets sounding, rode through the valley on their way to battle. Among them was a young soldier, a cousin of the shepherd-

boy, and not many years older. The boy
called to him and bade him good-bye; and
as the soldiers disappeared at the end of the
valley, he said to himself, " I wish I were
as old as my cousin, that I might go out to
fight the king's battles. He will risk his life
to help the king, and, may be, he may do
something great, and help to win a battle and
save our country; but I can do nothing but
stay here and watch these few sheep. I wish
I could do something to help the king."

As he said these words, a pigeon came
hurriedly flying close over his head. The
boy looked up, and there was a hawk chasing
after her. The poor bird flew round and
round, and here and there, and managed to
escape as far as the next meadow; but she
was close followed at every turn by the
hungry hawk, and it was clear she would be
caught in a minute if no help came. There
was no time to go round by the gate, so in a
moment the boy jumped on the high stone
wall that parted the two meadows; it was a
high wall, and there was a steep, rough rock

on the other side. The jump was a dangerous
one, but, without a moment's hesitation, the
brave lad leaped down; and the next moment,
though he sprained his foot and fell, striking
one cheek against a sharp edge in the rock, he
was up again on his feet, and, flinging his
crook at the hawk, he stopped him just in
time to save the poor trembling pigeon.

Then he took up the pigeon, more dead
than alive, and stroked it gently. In a few
minutes it seemed to gain strength and
courage. Meantime the shepherd-boy, limp-
ing as he went, carried the bird round to the
meadow where he was keeping his sheep. And
now, while he was feeding the pigeon with
some bread crumbs, it came into his mind,
" What am I to do with this pretty bird ? "
At first he said, " I will take it home to my
brothers and sisters. How pleased they will
be ! " Then it occurred to him, " Perhaps
the pigeon belongs to some one else : indeed,
it must, for it's not a wild wood-pigeon, but
a tame one, and besides, some one has tied a
silk thread and a piece of paper round its

neck. But then, have not I saved it? It would have been killed, but for me. Surely it belongs to me. And besides, if I let it go, may not another hawk kill it?" All this he thought to himself, and part of it he spoke aloud. But, when he had finished, his conscience told him that he ought not to keep the pigeon; it was very hard to let it go, but it was right, though hard. So he kissed the pigeon, and said, "Good-bye; go home to your master that gave you your little silk collar."

Away flew the pigeon, straight towards a castle at the top of a hill a long way off; and, at the same time, away galloped a man on horseback, down in the deep lane that ran by the side of the meadow. The boy wondered for a minute who it was that had been waiting quietly in the lane; but soon he forgot all about that.

Now you must know that this man waiting in the lane, who galloped off when the pigeon flew away, was no other than the king. The king had been riding a little way behind his soldiers, and had heard all the shepherd-boy's complaints, and how he wanted to do something to help the king. He had also noticed how the brave boy had jumped from the top of the high wall and had saved the pigeon. Moreover, just as the pigeon was rising to fly away, he had noticed the little piece of paper tied by the silk thread round the pigeon's neck. He had not noticed this while the bird was in the boy's hand, but, when it began to flap its wings, he caught sight of it, and then he knew at once that it was one of his own carrier pigeons bringing a note to his castle; and that was why, as soon as the pigeon flew off, the king galloped off as well, for he wanted to see what news the pigeon brought him. When he reached home, he saw the pigeon waiting for him; and, on opening the note, he found that it was from one of his generals, telling him where the enemy were encamped, and shewing him how he could bring up a fresh army, and so with the rest of his armies he might defeat the enemy.

About a month after this, when the shepherd-boy had almost forgotten all about the pigeon, back came the soldiers, again riding through the valley with the king at their head. And this time their trumpets sounded, not for war, but for gladness and peace; for they had defeated the enemy in a great battle, and now the war was over and the country was at peace.

Again the shepherd-boy looked at the brave soldiers riding through the valley to the king's castle, and again he wished that he had been a soldier able to do something to help the king. But, as wishing was no use, he tried to forget it, and to think only of his sheep and his work.

But next day, while he was sitting in the valley with his faithful dog by his side, came a messenger from the king, saying, "You are to come at once to the king's palace." The shepherd-boy could not believe it at first, and assured the messenger there must be some mistake; but the messenger said there was no mistake, and would not even give him time to put on his best clothes, but led him at once to the castle.

When they came into the castle hall, they found the king seated on his throne, and around him all his councillors, generals, and officers: and presently the trumpeter blew a trumpet and gave notice that he had been ordered to call out the names of all those that had helped the king in the war, and that each man was to answer to his name, and to come up to receive a reward.

So the trumpet blew, and the names were read out, and all that were called, both councillors and soldiers, went up in their fine robes to receive their rewards. At last the trumpet blew and the shepherd-boy's name was read out. At first he did not stir, for he felt sure there was some mistake, but those that were next to him said, "The king is looking at you: go up;" and they pushed him forward, and so he went up to the king, looking very much perplexed and a little ashamed. But the king smiled at him and said, "Little friend, what reward must I give you for the help you gave me in my war?" "Sir," said the shepherd-boy, " I deserve no reward, for I

have done nothing : I am only a poor shepherd-boy keeping a few sheep in the valley
yonder, and I could not help you, though I
wished it ever so much." "But," said the
king, uncovering a wicker cage, "I think you
know this bird; and are not you the brave
little boy that leaped down at the risk of his
life to save the pigeon from the hawk?" "I
saved the pigeon, sir; that is true." "Yes,
and afterwards you were honest enough to let
it fly again, instead of keeping it. Now this
pigeon brought me news that helped me to
gain the victory. So, you see, you helped me
without knowing it. Your reward shall be
this sword, and when you grow up I will make
you a captain in my army."

So the shepherd-boy in time became a soldier,
and lived to be a great general, and, before he
died, he had gained many battles, and had
done many brave deeds to help the king.

All little children are like that shepherd-
boy in the lonely valley. They have little

tasks and little duties; and it seems as though
they could not do anything great for God our
King. But, though it may seem so, it is not
so. No one knows whether what he is doing
is great or little. Very often an action that
seems very trifling is really great in God's
eyes. God our King takes note of all our
good actions, and He will reward us.

It seems a very little matter to be kind to
brothers and sisters, obedient to parents, and
industrious at lessons, just as it seemed to the
shepherd-boy a very little matter to watch over
a few sheep, and to be good and kind at home.
But if the shepherd-boy had not been good
and kind, and honest and brave in little things
before the pigeon came, he would not have
been so when it came, and then he would not
have helped the king. And so, if you are not
good in little things, you will find, when God
sends you some great thing to do, you cannot
be good in great things. Therefore, whatever
you do, whether alone or with others, whether
at work or in play, always remember that,
though you are a little child, you can do

P   I

something to help the King. You are helping Him whenever you are doing what is
right.

PASSING THE RIVER.

WO brothers were returning home
from a long journey, and came
to a stand at a deep, broad, dis-
mal-looking river. Mists and
fogs hung over the banks and
over all the water. Now and then the fog
broke a little, and they could catch a glimpse
of their pretty home high up upon a hill,
with the sunlight on the windows and on
the flowers. But this was not often; for the
most part the fog looked as solid as a wall,
and as black as night. They took off their
socks and dipped their feet in, and the water
was so cold that it made the younger brother
shudder all over. The elder brother was a
full-grown man; but the younger was only a
little boy, and he said, " I can never swim

across this horrible river, it is so cold as well as broad. And what if there are cruel, ugly monsters that eat men, swimming at the bottom; and one of them may catch us by the leg while we are swimming, and drag us under, and swallow us up in his big jaws? I dare not cross."

Then the elder brother said, "We must cross, for there is no other way to our father's home. Wait for me a moment." Then he plunged into the cold stream, and his head was covered with the water, and for a moment it seemed as though he were drowned; but he came up to the top, and swam boldly on. Soon he disappeared in the fog. Presently the little brother heard his voice on the other side, saying, "Never fear, plunge in." He answered, "I dare not; I am afraid." The voice said, "You must not be afraid. I have sounded the depth, and I know you cannot be drowned in it; and though it is very cold, I know you can bear it. Besides, it is not so broad as you think, and I shall be ready on the other side to help you out." "I wish I could see you," said the little brother. "That cannot be," said the voice, "for I see my father, and he tells me I must not come back to carry you over, because you can now swim for yourself. But I will come in some way, never fear."

So the little brother stepped in. And because he stepped in, instead of plunging boldly in, the water made him sob and shiver at first, and his knees shook, so that he felt he was going to lose his footing, and the rough water began to beat at his lips. But he heard his elder brother's voice saying, " Come on, never fear;" and he took courage and swam into the fog. And when he came to the deepest and roughest part of the river, he saw the form of his brother coming through the fog; and just when his arms began to be terribly tired, and he began to struggle as though he were sinking, his elder brother seized him by the hand and drew him to the shore; and there he found all was sunshine, and everywhere around were flowers and the songs of birds; and up above was the Father waiting to welcome him home.

The river is Death. Jesus is our Elder Brother, who has passed through Death, and His voice continually says to us, "Do not fear Death, for I have passed through it and know what it is: and I will help you across." God is our Father waiting for us on the other side.

LONDON:

R. CLAY, SONS, AND TAYLOR, PRINTERS,

BREAD STREET HILL.